FAIRY FARTS

Everything you never knew about flatulence in the fairy kingdom

written and illustrated by Kelli Hansen

This book is dedicated
to MKH,
who proves that even
the beautiful and graceful
sometimes have to let farts fly.

Everybody knows that fairies
are the most beautiful and
graceful creatures in the
entire magic world.

They flit and fly
with delicate sparkling wings,
and make magic
with their delightful dust.

But I am here to tell you
something no one knows.
It's the deep, dark secret
that the fairies
really, really, REALLY
don't want you to know.

You see,
most humans
have heard
of fairy dust,
but not too many
are aware of...

...fairy farts.
That's right.

ALL

FAIRIES

FART.

And although the fairies like to think
that their farts smell like roses and lilies,
the truth is...

...they don't.

You can understand why the fairies
want to keep the whole thing secret.
After all, they have a reputation of grace
and beauty to uphold. They usually
try their best to be discreet.

Unfortunately,
despite all the best fairy efforts,
sometimes their little secret
becomes obvious.

Really, I don't know what they expect,
especially when you consider
the typical fairy diet.
Everyone knows
that no true fairy can resist
a good bean burrito.

mmmm....

And don't even get me started on the fairy fascination with chili cook-offs.

Still, you can see how it could be
embarrassing,
no matter what the reason.

Most fairies just try to pretend
it doesn't happen.

The ice fairies have a
particularly difficult time with that.

They're not just embarrassing either.

They cause small problems
like fairy magic "backfires"
at best...

...and huge problems, like threats
to the whole fairy kingdom, at worst.

Despite the problems
it may cause, farting fairies
need to remember that
passing gas isn't all bad.

There are some perks.

hmmm...
like what, exactly?

For example, when a tired fairy
needs to fly fast, the force of air
can be quite helpful.

And as humans understand, farting is perfectly normal, and can be a whole lot of silly fun when you are with a friend who understands.

So now you know the stinky truth.
If ever you find yourself outside,
enjoying the natural world,
and you catch a whiff
of something slightly foul...

...you'll realize that you may
have just stumbled on the
magic of a fairy fart.

And although it may offend your nose,
just remember,
fairy farts make flowers grow...

Well.........
        maybe not.

THE END

Thank you for purchasing Fairy Farts!
Visit
www.findthewaypublishing.com/fairyfarts
to access
free printable coloring pages
featuring 3 new, unpublished "fairy farts"
scenes to color!

Made in the USA
Middletown, DE
23 December 2019